THE COPPER ECONOMY

CHUCK RYGG

DISCLAIMER

Acknowledgements

This book is dedicated to blue-collar workers everywhere who do hard physical labor in every kind of weather and regardless of whether they are sick, injured or well to provide a living for themselves and their families. Mike Rowe from the show "Dirty Jobs" says it best in the introduction to his show;

"I explore the country looking for people who aren't afraid to get dirty – hard-working men and women who earn an honest living doing the kinds of jobs that make civilized life possible for the rest of us. Now, get ready to get dirty."

The cover of this book, as well as this page uses the font Copperplate Gothic, because copper is the shit.

PREFACE

During the Gold Rush, a large group of people flooded into California with the hopes of getting rich, or at least, being better off than they were. Dreams of a better life and prosperity for their families motivated their decision to chase "The American Dream". Many people believe the Gold Rush fizzled out. This is far from the truth. It just changed commodities. Still, meager people look for precious metals in order to make ends meet. Scrappers collect aluminum and steel in many forms, but the most valuable is copper. Also known as "the poor man's gold," it fetches a high price and is readily available to those who know how to get it.

Ironically, while writing this novel, I was awoken in the small hours of the morning by the sound of a saw cutting metal, only to realize that a thief was cutting the copper down-spouts off a home across the street. This brash criminal grabbed the copper and made off with it into the night.

ONE

The Gang Box

Today was a day of mourning for some. Junior's dad had passed away and many of the residents had a lot of respect for the man who had taught them so much. They laid him to rest in the old cemetery that had many head stones bearing the family name. Junior stood next to a big white oak tree mourning his loss.

"My sincerest condolences Junior," said old man Bill.

"We wouldn't be here if my dad's dumbass helper had a voltage meter that worked," replied Junior.

They were trying to harvest the copper from that old building's electrical service right?" asked Bill.

"Yeah, something went wrong," answered Junior sadly.

"Your dad sure was a forty-niner. He could find that poor man's gold like nobody else. He took me a couple times. In one night, he would have the whole truck loaded down with copper wire and buss bars. We would cash it in the next day and not have to work for three months," said Bill.

"He was the greatest," said Junior.

"We're going to Mar-a-Lago for some beers. Do you want to come Junior?" asked Bill.

"No. I am going to go home and start taking care of things," replied Junior.

It was a warm summer day in "Welcome to Paradise Trailer Park." It only had a dozen trailers with large lots. Single family homes on four acre wooded lots surrounded most of the trailer park and were considered part of the same overall neighborhood. The residents were mainly working class people who were hard working and living folks. These were the type of people who would not pass up a chance to make a few extra bucks if the opportunity presented itself and they were always on the lookout for it. They usually got by pretty well, meaning nobody ever went hungry, but when their misery index got too high, it was nice to break the monotony of daily life with a trip to the local scrap yard, followed by some small luxury or necessity.

Junior went home to check out his departed father's tool shed that he was never allowed inside of, and for good reason. Junior's father had quite the work shed. Refrigerator for his beer, TV for watching NASCAR, and all the tools a man could hope for. As Junior sat there, drinking his father's beer one after another, he played with all the new tools, and finally got to the big orange gang box in the corner. This type of large metal box used on construction sites normally held tools and other materials and is locked up tight to keep the honest honest. It had four wheels under it, so when Junior tried to move it, he was surprised he couldn't. After staring at it for awhile, his curiosity forced him to take matters into his own hands. He went outside and walked directly to his four-wheel drive truck with the determination of a man who was finally promoted to foreman after taking orders and eating crow from management for far too long. Junior rigged-up a heavy lifting strap to the bumper and connected it to the gang box, hopped back in the truck and dragged it outside. The box had two padlocks on the front so he grabbed a drill from the vast array of tools that were now at his disposal, drilled out the cylinders and busted them off. As Junior threw open the top of the gang box and the sun hit the contents, a bright shining light came from within as if it were gold. Junior just stared in amazement. "Oh my god! I hit the lottery," he proclaimed out loud. He was staring at almost four thousand pounds of number one bright copper that his father had been saving. "Bare bright copper is over two dollars a pound. I'm rich! At good market value, it could be worth around nine thousand dollars." That would be a whole lot of money for a guy like him who barely makes that much that the government knew about in any given year.

It suddenly occurred to Junior that he was going to need to watch what he said and did so as not to attract attention. Much like a bottle of liquor, if somebody knows you have it, they are more than happy to indulge in it with you. Even though he had kin at the scrap yard nearby, he would have some explaining to do if the sheriff should come around. Cashing in a few hundred pounds now would be a good start and not look too suspicious he reckoned, although he wasn't the kind of guy who ever took much time to think things through.

Junior was a scatter-brained, tobacco chewing redneck who was always leaving tools around, misplacing his keys, and seldom bathed, which didn't help his big, goofy appearance. He could easily lose a hundred pounds and still not be considered thin. His doughy face had unremarkable features, and he wore the same clothes as he did in high school, including the Timberland boots that were a Christmas gift from his Aunt Violet. It would never dawn on Junior that keeping up with current fashions and being mindful of his eating habits might be a way to attract a girlfriend. Nonetheless, his kind, big-hearted nature was always noticed by friends and family who often described him as a man who didn't have a mean bone in his body.

He loaded up his booty and started out of the neighborhood only to stop and say "hi" to Miss Pritchett, the old lady who sat on her front porch at the entrance to the neighborhood and watched whoever came and went. Miss Pritchett's home was the definition of southern culture on the skids. It hadn't been painted since it was built, had a rusting refrigerator on the porch and the only thing that kept it from looking like a total mess was the nicely groomed front yard and the hand crocheted tablecloth on top of the refrigerator that kept the germanium plant from causing the rust from advancing too quickly. Miss Pritchett took pride in her crocheting and the fact that she lived in a real home and not one of the shitty trailers nearby. Her crochet hobby always made her look as if she was minding her own business and kept her hands busy, but she made professional spies look like they were asleep at the wheel. Nothing got by Miss Pritchett. Because Ms. Pritchett owned the building that Cindy's beauty shop was in, and if Cindy didn't stay in line, Ms. Pritchett would raise the rent. The old biddy had her "Aunt Bea" hair done for free as a "protection favor" from Cindy in return for letting her in on the local gossip and she liked the way Cindy did her hair.

"Hello Miss Pritchett," said Junior.

"Hi there, she replied. I'm so sorry to hear of your father. I always liked him."

"Thank you, that means a lot to me," said Junior.

Miss Pritchett saw the blinding light coming from the

back of the truck and asked, "Where you going with all that copper Junior?"

Junior replied, "I'm going to see my cousin down to the scrap yard. I can't sneak nothing past you can I? Please don't tell anyone you seed me with it ma'am."

"For my normal fee, my lips will be sealed," informed Miss Pritchett.

"OK. I'll give you twenty bucks when I get back," Junior said.

Then for no apparent reason Miss Pritchett blurted out, "I had relations with your father once after he cashed in a whole bunch of copper."

"I don't want to hear that you old bird," replied Junior.

"Well it's true," said Miss Pritchett.

"I feel sick now. I have to go. Goodbye Ma'am," Junior said with a little tip of his black NASCAR cap with the Chevy bow-tie on it. He didn't wear it too often on account of wanting to keep it nice, but grabbed it today without hesitation. After all, he was in mourning.

Junior pulled up at the scrap yard and was greeted by his cousin who went by the alias "Chrome Mags," but was often just called "Mags."

"Hey cousin! How you been? You haven't been here in a couple weeks, you must be broke by now," said Mags.

"I'm not broke. I have five one dollar bills," said Junior.

"Yeah and you only used two number two pencils in four

years of high school," replied Mags.

"What's everyone been bringing in lately?" Junior asked.

Chrome Mags pushed his CAT hat back from his forehead, and gave his dirty hair a scratch which sent a noticeable amount of debris dropping on his shoulder. "I've been getting beer cans, batteries, brake shoes, and some copper from refrigerator condensers today. Some guy dumped a little car out back. A Yugo," said Mags.

"What the hell is a Yugo?" asked Junior.

"I'm not sure but we have been throwing scrap steel at it all day," replied Mags. Jim got in it and Bob pushed him with the loader until he crashed into a refrigerator and broke a leg. Two whole weeks without an accident and we have a car wreck out back," said Mags.

"Man, I wish I got to drive it," said Junior.

"So what are you bringing in? More beer cans?" asked Mags

"Beer cans are worth about as much as Confederate money. I have something to show you," replied Junior.

"All you ever bring in is beer cans," said Mags.

"Yeah, I was broke Mags, but take a look at this," replied Junior as he let down the tail gate on the truck.

"Holy Shit - that's number one copper, said Mags. Where'd you git this?"

"Pop left it to me. What's the price today?" asked Junior.

"Two twenty-five a pound. Let's put it on the scale and run some numbers."

Junior started unloading the copper onto the scale when Mags announced officiously, "402 pounds, times two dollars, twenty-five cents per pound, so that comes to nine hundred four dollars and fifty cents."

Junior's heart almost skipped a beat. The five second rule just dropped to zero.

"I haven't had this type of cash in almost forever," Junior said, as he headed over to the cashier's window with Mags trailing close behind.

"Good. Maybe you can give me that twenty bucks you owe me," said Mags.

Junior looked sad. "This is grieving money. I need only buy the essentials," said Junior.

"Here is your money," said the cashier as she handed the money out of the hole in the bullet proof glass.

"I will talk to y'all later. I have supplies to get," said Junior.

Mags didn't press the issue on account of he was fond of Junior's old man too and sort of chalked it up to the cost of doing business even though he was as tough a scrap-yard guy as they come. Mags was a thirty-ish guy who always wore work gloves and who would win the dirtiest man in town contest every single time if there was such a thing. His clothes were not just filthy, they were a bio-hazard. They were so dirty that washing them would be pointless and this fact didn't bother him a bit because whatever he wore would just get dirty tomorrow.

The one big problem with the scrap yard was there were plenty of businesses all in a row to help you spend your new found fortune. The saying rich people plan for the next generation, middle class people plan for next year, and poor folks plan for what's happening on Saturday night, is entirely true. First came the liquor store. Junior thought to himself, "which was now."

Junior walked up to the counter at the Spirits of Calvert store and said, "30 pack of Bud Light, a fifth of Jack, and is that Dale Earnhardt Junior's flag hanging up there for sale?"

"That'll be forty one eighty for the beer and the liquor, but the Dale Junior flag is not for sale," replied the clerk.

"How about for a hundred bucks!" Junior asked.

"Sold, said the clerk. I'll roll it up so it don't get no hard creases in it."

"Much obliged," said Junior who was now feeling a whole lot better about himself.

The next store was the local convenience store. "Two cans of Copenhagen, a whole roll of them ten dollar scratch off tickets, and two multie-match lotto tickets. I feel lucky," Junior said to the clerk.

"Good Luck Sir," said the clerk as he handed Junior his change, receipt, and perhaps a new lease on life. Junior then stopped at the farm and garden store to pick-up some chicks for his coop and then he returned home, well pleased with all his purchases.

It was starting to get closer to evening so Junior lit a fire in the fire pit out in the yard which always attracted a few people. It wasn't long before Dwayne, a portly kind of guy, came pulling up on his four-wheeler. He always smelled like low-tide and being a waterman, had lots of character lines and wrinkles on his face from too much sun exposure on his crab boat. He was also missing part of his finger from a crab bite that got infected. Dwayne was a part-time crabber who trolled the Patuxent River near Benedict, MD where the water is warm from the discharge of the power plant. A proud veteran of the Navy, he enlisted at 18, served his 20 years, and retired two years ago.

"Hey, I saw your fire and came over for some beers," said Dwayne as he opened up the cooler strapped to his four wheeler.

"Great," said Junior.

"Real sorry to hear about your dad Junior. He was the best scrap man in this whole county," confided Dwayne.

"Thanks buddy," replied Junior.

"Did you see the wench car Reeb has? It's holdin' that engine block up in the air," said Dwayne.

"Yes, I did, said Junior. Looks like homemade ass, but Reeb can make anything."

Their neighbor, Reeb, or beer spelled backwards, was an auto mechanic that had rusted cars, scrap metal, and other debris covering almost every square inch of his yard. Part of his yard was known as "the waste land." It was scorched earth from a tire fire that had burned for a week straight. Although he didn't appear to be particularly bright, he had a kind of red-neck ingenuity that garnered him respect from the working poor in the community. People took notice when he attached a steel cable to a car rim on a 65' Impala that was jacked-up in his yard. The steel cable went through a couple pulleys on a big steel tripod. All he had to do was attach it to a load and hit the gas so the steel cable would wind it up in the air.

Reeb was a very talented car mechanic whose clothes were stained with oil and strong hands permanently embedded with grease. He wasn't bad looking if you could overlook his ratty beard, bad dental work, and the fact that he obviously cut his own hair.

"I'm not sure how you live across from that guy with all that crap in his yard. His son's got lockjaw from Tetanus. Poor boy!"

"Oh you don't like Reeb?" asked Junior

"I'm not sayin' I wouldn't go fishing with the man, replied Dwayne. Oh, he's coming over."

"Hey guys! Who's got a beer for Reeb?"

"Here you go," said Dwayne.

"How's your boy's lock-jaw?" asked Junior in a friendly, well meaning way.

"It's gettin' better. I see you got some new chickens. Good lookin' birds Junior," said Reeb, who was now tipsy enough to start getting on his soap box.

"Did y'all give any thought to my Ocean's Eleven style copper heist on the Statue of Liberty?" asked Reeb.

"Man, the only symbol you know on the periodical table

of elements is copper and aluminum," said Dwayne.

"What's your plan? Cut it down and float it down the river?" asked Junior.

"If you polished that french lady up you couldn't look at her unless you had a welding mask on," said Dwayne.

"We could get jobs working there and loosen every bolt on the statue so one night you turn the lights out and finish the job," said Reeb.

"I draw the line there. Get a job. Hell no!" said Junior.

"If we pulled it off we wouldn't have to work ever again," said Reeb.

"I barely work now," said Junior.

"Don't sell yourself short Junior. You do work hard sweeping the parking lot of the liquor store," said Dwayne.

"I just keep thinking about that statue," said Reeb.

"Like that stupid plan to go down to that author's house down the street and steal his Sherman tank for scrap steel?" said Junior.

"It was an idea," replied Reeb.

"What is his name?" asked Junior

"Tom Clancy. He was a Navy man like me," said Dwayne.

"I think someone would figure it out if you came in the scrap yard with pieces of a tank," said Junior.

"The hunt for redneck dumb asses would be a lot easier

than finding a Russian sub," said Dwayne.

"Just keep thinking about that statue," said Reeb.

"I been thinking about the traffic every time I have to leave the county," said Dwayne.

"Yeah, pretty soon if you don't live within five miles of where you work you're probably going to be late," said Junior.

"I hate people who drive the speed limit in the damn left lane," said Reeb.

"The beltway is a crazy place. People with beds and furniture flying off of their cars like a bunch of idiots," said Dwayne, who was always glad to vent his frustrations about the traffic up north.

"Oh and you give me crap for NASCAR only turning left. That section in Montgomery County has left and right turns and they start crashing at 5 AM everyday," said Junior.

"95, 495, Route 66, and 270 are brought to you by the maker of brake shoes, I tell you," said Dwayne in his announcer voice.

"Are you two going to have your Redskins/Cowboys rivalry in full speed soon?" asked Junior.

"You know we are," said Reeb.

In this part of the world, if the Redskins beat the Cowboys you would think they won the championship. It was that important.

Dwayne said, "If I had any motivation at all, I would get into the junk hauling business."

Reeb replied, "Yeah - get paid twice. Picking up the junk and then for selling it. Sometimes all they have is junk, but they ask you to haul a lot of stuff away that is worth money at the scrap yard."

"My dad didn't teach me to throw away money," said Junior.

"That's how you live off the land," said Reeb.

"It's small scores like that that make life easier." said Dwayne.

Junior and Reeb both nodded. They knew this was their way of life.

"Yup. Hey can y'all help me put up my new flag?" said Junior, as he grabbed the Dale Jr. flag out of the truck.

They ran it up the flag pole and admired it in the light of the fire.

"Is that the one from the liquor store?" asked Dwayne.

"Hell to the yeah!" said Junior.

"New chickens. New flag. Where you gettin' all this loot?"asked Reeb.

Junior crushed another beer can and said with a slow, slurred voice, "My father left me some number one."

"Good for you! Was it a lot?" asked Dwayne.

"A shit load. I got it locked up in that gang box over there. I'm set for a long while."

Junior was as drunk as three people and accidentally shot

his mouth off. Somewhere in his drunken, grieving mind, he knew that having had too much to drink and running your mouth is a bad idea when you're talking about number one copper.

Reeb, with a juicy new piece of information, quickly changed the subject.

"Why don't y'all settle a debate for me," Reeb said. I say that 75% of the county's residents have eaten squirrel."

"85%," said Junior.

"We have a lot of people moving south that haven't. 70%," said Dwayne.

"I'm sticking with 85%. Just cause you have money don't mean you don't like squirrel," said Junior as he turned and blew a snot rocket on the ground.

"Muskrat is pretty good eatin'," said Reeb.

"Do you put Old Bay Seasoning on Muskrat?" asked Junior.

"Come on man. Old Bay goes on everything," said Dwayne.

"I'm going to pass out. I'll see you guys later," said Junior.

"Take it easy," said Dwayne.

Reeb and Dwayne said their goodbyes and looked at each other. They went back to their houses knowing that it was only a matter of time before one of them went for the gang box.

TWO

STICKY FINGERS

Much like a prospector in 1849, who looked for precious gold in a total frenzy, a similar "get rich quick" feeling came over Reeb. As he sat in his dark house staring out the windows watching Dwayne and Junior's houses, his cocky, drunken mind reassured him that he was well within his right to get ahead. He saw Dwayne's lights go out and Junior's house was still dark and quiet. "It's time to go," thought Reeb as he walked into his sons bedroom and woke him up. "Come on boy we have work to do."

They crept outside and Reeb explained the plan. "Okay we have to let-down the engine block off the lift onto a dolly and get it out of the way. I want you to take the steel cable off the upper reel, pull it across the street, and attach the hook to that gang box. I only want to have the car running for a few minutes," said Reeb.

"Okay Dad," said Johnny in his funny lockjaw voice.

Reeb put the car in neutral and Johnny put the engine on the dolly and pushed it away from the rear of the car as Reeb got the cable off of the top pulley. He started feeding the cable off the wheel of the car to his son as Johnny pulled the cable across the street. Johnny wrapped the cable around the gang box handle and hooked it, then he climbed on top and held the cable to make sure it wouldn't come off. He waved to his dad that he was ready and Reeb hopped in the car. He grabbed the screwdriver that he used to start it, stuck it in the steering column, started the car, and hit the gas. The gang box popped a little wheelie and took off across the street doing 20 miles an hour. Johnny held on for dear life, lying on his stomach and gripping the sides of the box as best he could. When the gang box careened into the yard, Reeb slammed on the brakes but the gang box kept rolling. It hit the rear of the car sending Johnny flying over the car and onto the hood. He landed spread eagle on his back with a thud that was hard enough to spill the change from his front pockets in a cascade over the car hood. "We're in the money now Johnny," said Reeb who was making light of his son's little accident to lighten-up the mood. Johnny instinctively started picking up his loose change only to suddenly halt when his father said, "Get it later boy. Come on get over here and help me roll it behind the stack of tires. We can get a car hood or two to help finish covering it up."

Dwayne watched the two through his living room picture window with a night vision monocle.

"It's too heavy Dad, grunted Johnny, it's like pushing a broke down car."

"We can do this. Now push damnit!" ordered Reeb. The two struggled to get it behind a stack of tires.

"Alright. Now grab a car hood and cover it up on the sides so nobody can see it," said Reeb.

"What's in it?" asked Johnny.

"The one thing I love more than beer," said Reeb.

"Oh, you mean copper?" asked Johnny.

"Enough to buy a couple years worth of beer ha-ha-ha,

said Reeb. Tomorrow morning I want your ass up bright and early loading up the truck so we can get to the scrap yard, so go get some sleep."

"OK Dad. Goodnight," replied a tired and banged -up Johnny.

When the commotion was over and Reeb and Johnny plodded back to the house, Dwayne waited patiently for Reeb's light to go out. He quickly grabbed his cordless drill and sneaked outside to the big gray trash can on wheels near the driveway. He started toward Reeb's house, dragging the trash can behind him, trying to be as quiet as possible. Dwayne had a distinctive walk because of a limp he had from falling off of a ladder trying to steal some rich guy's copper gutters, which made him easily identifiable to Ms. Pritchett, even in the dark, who was watching his every move. She smiled at the absurd antics she just witnessed as she dropped a couple Alka Seltzers into a glass of water. She thought to herself "this is gonna be good," as she settled into her chair behind the living room curtains, sipping her remedy, and for once, she wasn't so perturbed about all the fried chicken and collard greens she ate for dinner coming back on her with a vengeance.

Dwayne moved the car hoods and quickly drilled out the cylinders on the locks, opened up the gang box, and started filling up the trash can with the copper. He then shut the gang box and put the car hoods back where they were. He slowly rolled back to his yard and put a lid on the trashcan so no one would know what was inside. He was careful to park it right over the spot where he always kept it, which was an easy alignment due to the sharp outline of dead grass. He crept back into the house in slow motion making sure the screen door didn't slam as he entered. All that fresh air made him hungry, so he made his way into the kitchen to make a sand-wich. Almost forgetting he was in "stealth mode,"he went to switch on the kitchen light. Stopping himself, he opened the refrigerator instead, and rooted around for some bologna and american cheese. He left the door ajar just enough to give him some light to slap together his midnight snack. "Won't Reeb be pissed when he finds out he ain't as smart as he thinks he is," thought Dwayne. An evil little smile came over his face as he choked down the sandwich and then made his way to bed.

Back across the street, Ms. Pritchett figured her neighbor-hood watch shift ended, so she put her glass by the bathroom sink, kicked-off her slippers and climbed back into bed. As she relaxed on the deluxe pillow-top mattress she had gotten as a payment for some high jinx she witnessed a few years back, she thought about how she might enrich herself from tonight's little caper. She really wanted a new crock-pot, but then realized she ought to raise her ambitions. After all, we're talking about copper, she said to herself, already rehearsing the speech she was planning on giving the village idiots. Feel-ing a might guilty for her greedy nature, she contented herself by saying, "Oh that poor lockjaw boy. God bless him."

Early the next morning in the pre-dawn light, Johnny wandered out into the yard and saw that the gang box had been tampered with and ran back inside the house.

"DAD, DAD, DAD someone's been inside the box," Johnny hollered hysterically.

"God damn it, Reeb shouted. Let's go!"

They ran outside and jumped into the truck. They tried to start it, but it would only crank.

"Shit," said Reeb.

"Some mechanic," said Johnny.

"Let's get the car," said Reeb.

Their car was a 90's model Saturn that had too many miles and years on it, had big spots of cancer rust, but it still ran. Reeb fired it up, backed it up next to the gang box, and popped the trunk.

"Put as much in as you can Johnny," ordered Reeb. As they started filling the trunk, the weight of the copper on the rear shocks started to make it sag noticeably.

"Oh shit! Junior's coming!" Reeb exclaimed. I'll try to distract him."

Johnny closed the gang box and the trunk and jumped in the driver's seat.

"Hey Junior," said Reeb in his neighborly way.

"Where the hell is my gang box? Somebody stole it and when I find him I am going to beat the shit out of him", said Junior.

"Oh calm down man, I haven't seen it. I was just about to take Johnny to a lock-jaw appointment," said Reeb.

"Somebody stole my inheritance and he'll have hell to pay," said Junior in a voice that was part sorrow, part anger, and mostly desperation.

Just then their neighbor Mike came out of his trailer to water his flowers. Mike's yard was perfectly manicured with nice flower beds and perfect grass, only problem was it bordered Reeb's yard.

"Mike have you seen my gang box?" yelled Junior.

"No, I haven't, replied Mike, all I see is trash and filth when I look in that direction. Keep your trash from getting in my yard Reeb."

"You want to see trash Mike?" responded Reeb.

Reeb grabbed a brake shoe and put it in the basket of a small catapult and launched it over the fence, almost hitting Mike.

"You animal! You shouldn't be allowed to live amongst regular people," yelled Mike.

"Up yours Mike! Junior, we gotta go or we'll be late to the doctor's. I'll look out for that gang box and help you when I get back", said Reeb.

"Thanks man," said Junior who didn't realize he was standing less than ten feet from it.

Reeb hopped into the passenger seat and ordered his son to kick it in the ass. Johnny hit the gas, but the hesitation on the Saturn could be clocked in five seconds.

"Not exactly what I'd call a burn-out Johnny," said Reeb in his redneck, dead-pan voice.

"Lighten-up Dad, replied Johnny, what do you expect from this hoop-D?"

"Not a hell of a lot son, replied Reeb. Damnation! Miss Pritchett! Slow down John-boy."

Johnny crawled the car up to where Miss Pritchett was standing and his father leaned out of the window.

"Well good day to you Miss Pritchett, what's up?" asked Reeb in his neighborly way.

"A rooster's ass when he eats, replied Miss Pritchett. You have a one hundred dollar fine from me for what you did to poor Junior last night."

Reeb, trying to dispense with the matter as quickly as he could, replied, "One hundred dollars? Don't have that on me Miss Pritchett."

"Well you have four hours before I release the hounds on you, so you better get busy," Miss Pritchett ordered.

"Four hours! But I'm leaving the County. Johnny's got a lock jaw appointment. You know what traffic is like up there," said Reeb.

"Four hours!" said Miss Pritchett.

"OK you old biddy, we gotta go!" said Reeb.

Johnny tromped on the gas and as they accelerated, a cloud of dust enveloped Miss Pritchett.

"You keep a civil tongue in your head Reeb!" hollered Miss Pritchett, but all Johnny and Reeb could hear was something that sounded like Dino's bark from the Flintstones underneath the sound of the Saturn's chewed-off exhaust system.

"Johnny, we've been found out by that crazy old lady," said Reeb.

"Do you think she is going to sick the chicks on us?"

asked Johnny.

"More than likely son, replied Reeb. That cunning old bat will blackmail anybody to get her share. She lives on the same street as the President of the United States and both of them have their hands in your pockets."

"What time do we need to be at the doctor's?" asked Johnny.

"What doctors?" Reeb said.

"My lock jaw doctor Dad," replied Johnny.

"You'll live boy," said Reeb.

Johnny was a little more confused than usual, but decided to just follow his Dad's direction. He thought about his health care very infrequently, but started to worry that maybe his father was starting to care more about copper than he was for him. He knew his Dad loved him. Caring for his well-being was another thing and something his father wasn't too good at. All the same, Johnny soon forgot about the fake appointment and was glad that he and his father could spend some quality time together.

"Son, we need to get the copper sold and back here in less than four hours so I can pay Miss Pritchett," said Reeb.

"When are you going to take me to the doctor's?" asked Johnny

"When we cash in the rest of that gold," replied Reeb

Reeb's plan was to drive the copper to a scrap yard a couple counties away so it would not be detected by Chrome

Mags or anyone that he knows. They pulled into the Brandywine scrap yard and unloaded the copper onto the scale.

"Five hundred eighty pounds at two dollars and twenty five cents a pound. That comes to one thousand three hundred five dollars," said the scrap yard man.

"I wonder what the poor people are doing tonight," said Reeb.

"God damn! Real money!" yelled Johnny.

They jumped back in the car and started to make their way back down south, but the car started spitting and sputtering as it slowly grinded to a halt.

"We've only been gone two and a half hours and now this," said Reeb.

"But we're rich Dad," said Johnny.

"There's a lot more at the house, so stay focused boy," said Reeb.

They started to work on the car and Johnny could see a couch that had fallen off of someone's truck by the side of the road.

"When we get the car fixed, do you want to harvest that couch?" asked Johnny.

"We don't have time for that bullshit son. Like I said, stay focused!" replied Reeb.

"Well it was just an idea. We could sell it at the flea market this weekend," offered Johnny.

"If we weren't sitting on so much copper I would say yes, but right now, hell no!" replied Reeb.

After getting the car started again, Reeb made a surgical strike at the local butcher shop and loaded up on big t-bone steaks, chips, junk food and beer as if he was late to a hurricane party.

THREE

Posh

Cindy was an enterprising woman and owner of the Posh Hair & Nail Salon. The salon did a steady business with all the local women and was a corner-stone of the female community. Cindy came up with the name because she was a big fan of the Spice Girls in her teenage years and "Posh Spice" was her favorite girl. She also thought it gave the simple, small salon an upscale kind of sound and the local women appreciated her for the warm and caring atmosphere. The Spice Girls poster Cindy hung up by the hair washing station also served to remind all the women of their high school glory days.

Cindy cared more about how her customer-friends were doing and feeling, rather than what they were doing, or with whom. All of her loyal customers knew they could trust her, and as a result, confided some of their most intimate problems and life experiences to her. She listened more than she spoke, but when she did speak, everyone knew she had something wise and important to say. Cindy had heard it all. The best and the worst of human behavior came to her ears and nothing shocked or surprised her anymore. Posh wasn't just "Vegas" in terms of confidentiality, it was a bank vault and a confessional rolled into one. Like all salons, it had strict rules. Anybody telling tales out of school, embellishing the facts, or just being a bitch would be called down. No cell phones, no catty remarks against other customers unless they were "out of towners", and most important of all, no back-stabbing Cindy. No woman would ever dare to do that, but the one woman who trash-talked her ended up with the most unbecoming hair color imaginable and a hair style that took two years to grow out properly. She also got charged twice and much as Cindy's normal prices, but she paid it, and slinked out of the salon in a "walk of shame" the women of the town will never forget. You just don't go up against your own hair dresser unless you want to look like a damn fool for a long, long time. The humiliation never seemed to end for the woman who broke the rules, especially when her husband said "what did you do to your hair" the moment she entered the house. The punishment was far worse than the crime, but Cindy wanted the woman not to forget that they were all trying to run a civilization.

Marylou and Nancy Victoria, A.K.A., N.V. were both waitresses at Mar-A-Lago Tavern, a grimy bar and grill down the road a piece from Posh. They always got appointments at the same time to get their hair done so they could visit with their mutual high school friend Cindy, catch-up on the local news, and discuss their personal problems, successes, and challenges. N.V., the hottest blonde in town, had root touch-ups more often than women usually do because she was convinced everybody thought she was a "natural blonde." Marylou on the other hand was a brunette, too young to have any grey hair, and who had beautiful, shiny, thick, long hair. Although Marylou had "girl next door" looks, and lacked N.V.'s hotness, she had a cute figure and the map of Ireland on her face. Everyone loved Marylou's wholesome, good looks, but she didn't know that since her side-kick always got all the attention. N.V., on the other hand was a little rough around the edges with a little man hating attitude and latched onto the southern bell from the trailer park, Marylou, who was the perfect opposite and easy to push around. There was no question N.V. was a very good looking girl - tall, blonde, and not to be trusted around your boyfriend.

"Well hey Cindy! You workin' hard or hardly working," announced N.V when she and Marylou came through the salon door.

"Right back at you," replied Cindy with a big smile and a hug. "How you doin' ladies?"

As usual, N.V. spoke for both she and Marylou, replying "Oh just ducky."

"You sure about that?" asked Cindy.

"I'm not sure about anything," Marylou replied.

"Now I know something's up, said Cindy. You're lookin' a little pale hon. Your friend visiting?"

"Yeah and she's a bitch" confided Marylou.

"Go on help yourself to some Midol from that drawer under the register and put your feet up for awhile," offered Cindy.

"Thanks Cindy, I could surely use some."

Marylou washed a couple tablets down with a Dr. Pepper, and settled into the big reclining pedicure chair while N.V. was getting her hair washed.

"Oh Cindy, I feel better already," sighed Marylou.

Miss Pritchett ran the chicks like a mob boss. She had Cindy gathering information from the local women at the nail salon, and Marylou and N.V. right down the street at the Mar-A-Lago Tavern listening to chit chat as people ate. Miss

Pritchett's house was ideally located adjacent to Posh, and N.V.'s trailer was within shouting distance. She had known the girls all their lives and was looked at as a mother figure. She watched the neighborhood and knew when people would be home and could get the girls in action, as needed. She knew only a couple people were home that day and was watching the clock in case Reeb didn't make the timeline she set.

Back in the salon, Cindy toweled off Marylou's hair as the women settled down for a chat.

"Would you date Dale?" asked Cindy.

"Hell no! He's always broke. John maybe. He has a boat," said N.V.

"John doesn't have much money. Spends it all on the boat," Cindy stated.

"Yeah, but he still has a boat to take me out on," said N.V.

"You're going to get your heart broken like that," informed Cindy.

"Not if I break his first," said N.V. confidently.

Cindy reached into the pocket of her smock and grabbed her ringing phone.

"Hi Miss Pritchett," said Cindy.

"Reeb is late with a payment and I need you to do a job for me," said Miss Pritchett.

"What's in it for us?" asked Cindy as she shot a knowing look at N.V.

"Could be worth a lot of money," said Miss Pritchett.

"I'm listening," replied Cindy.

"Junior is out in his tool shed. Get N.V. to distract him so you can look inside of an orange gang box in Reeb's yard. I think it's full of copper. Check it out and let me know," said Miss Pritchett.

"Copper! You sure about that Miss Pritchett?" asked Cindy.

"I'm never wrong," replied Miss Pritchett.

"You're right about that," said Cindy as she tried to humor Miss Pritchett and stay on her good side. If there was a good side. "We're on it."

Cindy put her phone away and rallied the girls.

"N.V. - go home and put on your Daisy Duke's and those sexy boots you just got and keep Junior from going in his front yard," directed Cindy.

"OK. What's going on with that fool?" asked N.V.

"Well Miss Pritchett said there's a whole lot of copper in a gang box," said Cindy.

"Copper! Oh goody!" exclaimed N.V. I've got a cute top that shows off my boobs to go with it," said N.V. as she ran out the door.

"That'll work," replied Cindy with a little laugh as she resumed Marylou's blow-out.

"Me too," said Marylou who was a little relieved that she

wasn't being called into the plot at the moment.

N.V.'s trailer was no more than fifty yards away from Junior's place, so it didn't take long before she was changed and on her way to visit Junior. She slowed down her pace as she approached the door of the tool shed and rapped a couple times.

Junior flung open the door and saw a sight for sore eyes as his jaw dropped open a little.

"Hi sweetie," said N.V.

"Oh hello N.V. How are you doing today?" asked a startled Junior.

"I understand you got some new baby chicks. Can I see them?" asked N.V.

"Sure thing. They're out back in the coop. Give me one second," said Junior as he went back into the tool shed to look for something to make him smell a little better. He rooted around in a drawer and pulled out a decrepit looking bottle of Old Spice, slapped some on his face and wiped his hands on his shirt before rejoining N.V. in the yard.

"After you," said Junior as he opened the back gate.

"You smell good Junior. Sexy," said N.V.

"Thank you. The chicks are right here," Junior said as he opened the door to the coop.

"They are adorable," coo'd N.V as she picked one up and held it to her cleavage.

Junior's jaw started dropping open again as he watched

N.V. pet the little chick.

Once Cindy watched them go out back, she walked down the road, looked around a little, and ran into Reeb's yard. She located the gang box and opened the lid.

"OH SHIT! I think I just had a little orgasm," thought Cindy.

She let the lid of the box slam and ran out of the yard. Miss Pritchett caught sight of her and gave her a call.

"Well what does it look like?" asked Miss Pritchett.

"It looks like I could get a new pair of boobs, replied Cindy. Let me work on this some more and I will call you back."

"KEEP HIM BUSY!" appeared on N.V.'s phone as she cuddled the little chicks.

"Go into the tool shed out of sight until I tell you to come back out," said the next text.

"Who's that Cindy?" asked Junior.

"Oh just my idiot boss asking me to come in a half hour early today," lied N.V.

"Oh," said Junior.

Cindy re-entered the salon and asked Marylou what time she had to be at work.

"4:30, said Marylou. Mr. Chang wants us there a half hour early today to fill up the salt and pepper shakers with packets from McDonald's today."

"Jesus Christ Marylou, said Cindy. How come you can't

get a better job? You're smart."

Marylou just continued gazing at herself in the mirror and wondered the same thing.

"He can't figure out why he isn't making a profit when business is always so good," said Marylou.

"So he's thinks he can make it up by having you girls doing slave labor? He's a little asian dick making you do that crap, said Cindy. We gotta bring in the heavy artillery. I need you to call Jeff and sweet talk him into moving that gang box from Reeb's yard. The old bird was right once again."

"What's in the box?" asked Marylou

"Poor man's gold and lots of it. Saw it with my own eyes. I bet we could make some jewelry for the fair with some of the scraps too," replied Cindy.

"That would be fun!" said Marylou.

"Let's do that, but not today. We have to hurry and get it picked-up. It's in Reeb's front yard. Can you call Jeff and John and get them to move it?" asked Cindy.

"Sure Cindy, replied Marylou. Piece of cake. I'll get them moving."

Marylou quickly called Jeff. "Jeff sweety....Can you do me a favor? You in the roll-back today?" asked an upbeat Marylou.

"Sure thing cutie pie. What is it?," said Jeff.

"I need you to go to Reeb's house and pick-up a gang box from his front yard. Drop it behind the Mar-A-Lago Tavern out back by the dumpsters for me, OK?" asked Marylou.

"What's in it for us?" asked Jeff.

"Dinner's on me and a little kiss," offered Marylou.

"How do you still have a job if you keep giving away all the food, but we'll do it," said Jeff.

"I know, but you let me worry about that. OK?" replied Marylou.

"I do a lot of work because you have a crush," said Jeff.

"Whatever," said Marylou trying to sound as bored as possible.

"We'll swing by Reeb's in about 15 minutes," promised Jeff.

"Works for me," replied Marylou.

N.V. walked Junior back to the shed. "Do you have any beer in there?" asked N.V.

"I sure do," said Junior.

"Want to hang out and have a few with me?" asked N.V. as she walked to the shed.

"Oh my god yes," replied Junior.

N.V. could hear the sound of a big truck in the distance and knew that was her cue.

"Junior, does that radio work?" asked N.V.

"Yes it does," said Junior as he switched it on.

"Turn it up! said N.V., Let's dance!"

"I love this song," said Junior.

Junior lumbered over to N.V. and slapped both hands on her hips as they started to dance to the slow country song. N.V. immediately grabbed both of Junior's hands and replanted them up on her waist.

"Sorry," said Junior.

Jeff and John pulled into the trailer park and quickly backed into Reeb's driveway.

"This guy has a lot of crap," said John.

"I found it!" said Jeff. Give me the hook so we can pull it up and strap it down. We aren't getting paid by the hour."

Cindy saw the roll-back load up and cruise past her shop window and texted N.V. the "all clear." The shed door flew open.

"I'm not doing that with you! yelled N.V. The last time I kissed you I was pickin' tobacco out of my teeth for a week."

"I thought we were getting along," said Junior.

"Dream-on Junior," said N.V. as she stormed off.

Jeff and John pulled in behind Mar-A-Lago Tavern and off-loaded the box as Marylou came out of the kitchen door.

"Thank you so much," said Marylou.

"You wanna go see a movie with me?" asked Jeff.

"Maybe some other time," replied Marylou knowing he was going to ask as she quickly walked into the kitchen door.

"Let's go get some beers," said John quickly in an attempt to save Jeff's ego.

"Not gettin' any lovin' so might as well, replied Jeff. Let's haul that tulip poplar down to the Amish saw mill for Charlie so I'm at my thirstiest when we get back." The guys pulled out of the parking lot and headed down the road.

Reeb & Johnny came home after scrapping & shopping.

"What the hell! The box is gone! Son of a bitch!" hollered Reeb.

"Easy come, easy go," replied Johnny.

"That old woman got us again and I paid her anyway. We got to get this figured out," said Reeb.

FOUR

MAR-A-LAGO

With some it's "happy hour", with others it's unhappy hour at the Mar-A-Lago Tavern. Junior still crying in his beer over the missing gang box. John and Jeff for still not getting anywhere with the ladies, but for a bar keeper that pays attention, means a lot.

"I will kill whoever stole that gang box from me," proclaimed Junior in a sloppy half-drunken slur.

"Are you serious? You say it was filled all the way up with #1 Bright Copper?" asked Drake.

"Does a bear shit in the woods?", said Junior.

"That must have been worth a fortune. I've never seen that much. What was it like?", asked Drake.

"It shined like the sun! Made me get emotional. I thought of life, liberty, and the way you feel when you see The Blue Angels when they come to Annapolis, you know," said Junior.

"Don't worry Junior, It's all still out there. You just have to find it. John and Jeff just showed up. I have to go get these guys some beers. I'll be back later," said Drake.

Drake went to the other end of the bar.

"Hey - what have y'all been doin' tonight?", asked Drake.

"Wonderin' what it's going to take to get them girls to give us some lovin'," Jeff said sadly.

"They have us do stuff for them and it doesn't get us anywhere," said John.

"What did they have you do?", asked Drake as he poured them a couple beers.

"We went and moved a gang box for them and put it behind the tavern. God damn thing was heavy as shit," said John.

"Is that right? Y'all put it behind the tavern? Beer's on me boys. I'll be right back. I gotta phone call to make, and hopefully when I get back you two won't be looking so pitiful," said Drake.

"We're already drinking for free" said Jeff, once Drake was out of ear shot.

John looked up at the ceiling as if he was searching for divine salvation and said, "I know."

"Hey Bubba - it's Drake. I need you to do something for me. There's a gang box I want you to pick-up and drop it off in the holler behind my house."

"What's the job pay?" asked Bubba.

"A weeks worth of free beer at the bar and a bottle of Jack," Drake replied.

"I'm on it, said Bubba, where's it at?"

"Behind Mar-A-Lago Tavern," said Drake.

Bubba repo'd cars for a living, sometimes for money and sometimes for favors. He lived in the small black community located behind the Baptist Church, and had a wife and three kids who were always growing out of their clothes. A weeks worth of free beer and whiskey meant he didn't need to dip into the grocery money for his sin. It was summer-time and Bubba enjoyed an afternoon nap after church in the shade of the one tree in his yard, and then do some fishing with his boys. Bubba had a friendly face that counter-balanced his intimidatingly huge build.

"Yeah, that's what I'm going to do," thought Bubba as a little smile came across his face. The chores were going to have to wait this Sunday and Bubba's wife Velma knew her hard working husband deserved some down-time, especially in summer, since it helped make up for all the freezing nights he spent going all over hell's half-acre scooping up cars from their dead-beat owners.

Bubba hopped in his roll-back truck and was at Mar-A-Lago Tavern in just a few minutes. He pulled the gang box up onto the truck with the winch, strapped it down, and headed for Paradise Trailer Park. Rapid response was his forte' and he wasn't about to pass up the opportunity to get a weeks worth of all he could drink beer.

Marylou came out of the kitchen. "Hey boys, I bought you a pound of steamed shrimp for doing me that favor."

"Thank you!" said John.

"Y'all let me know if you need anything else, OK?" said Marylou.

Marylou turned around and bent over moving the beers around and making sure they had plenty of ice on them.

"Oh my god!" said Jeff who was staring at her thong sticking out of her jeans.

N.V. came out of the kitchen and saw Jeff staring at her butt so she walked up and put her hand on Marylou's butt saying, "Looks good huh boys?"

"Ooooh," said Marylou.

"Oh yeah," said Jeff.

John just stood staring.

"Did you tip your waitress?" asked N.V.

The two guys started going through their pockets looking for money then threw a couple five dollar bill on the bar.

"Cindy is calling," said N.V.

"Hey girl," said Cindy.

"Where have you been?" asked N.V.

"I had a client come in or I would have been there by now," replied Cindy.

"We have to get on this before someone figures out what we did," said N.V.

"Have you seen it yet?" asked Cindy.

"Hold on a minute," as she walked through the kitchen and out the back door.

"I don't even see it," said N.V.

"What?" replied Cindy.

"Marylou!" yelled N.V.

Marylou ran out of the back door.

"What?" she replied.

"The box isn't here," said N.V.

"I have to go," said N.V. as she hung up on Cindy.

"Where the hell is it!" Marylou exclaimed. Realizing she said it out loud, she raised the back of her hand to her mouth and thought, "I keep getting them idiots to do things and it never goes right. Well what can I expect giving a job this important to a couple of big dumb-asses like those two. What was I thinking?"

"Let's go talk to them N.V. and make it nice and clear that this is pretty far from OK with us," Marylou said.

"When do you want to talk to them?" asked N.V.

"Well right now would be a good time. Don't you think N.V.?" said Marylou.

"I guess you're right. Those two guys need some motivation." replied N.V.

"Uh-huh," Marylou replied with a nod of her head and a smirk on her face., "Those two little shits aren't stringing us along."

Marylou and N.V. straightened-up their uniforms, regained their composure, and walked back through to the bar like they didn't have a care in the world. With their best sweet southern charm, they both descended on Jeff and John's table like they were on a mission from god. N.V reached down to freshen-up the bar. Meantime, Marylou smiled at the boys and said, "How you guys doing? Need anything?"

Jeff and John straightened up in their chairs hoping this was the moment they had been waiting for.

"Ah no Marylou We're doin' just fine. How bout you?" asked John.

"Well I'd be doing a whole lot better if you two hadn't just drunk a beer a piece and ate a pound of shrimp," replied Marylou coldly.

"What's the matter baby?" asked a befuddled Jeff.

"Don't call me baby." replied Marylou.

"I'm sorry," John quickly said fearing he might have ruined his chances.

"How come you two think you're so special you can come in here and soak-up our hospitality without doing the one thing we asked you to do?" Marylou said in a confrontational voice.

"Whadda-ya-mean Marylou?" replied John, who now felt like he spoke for the both of them. "We put it out back this morning."

Jeff just sat still, but managed to nod in the affirmative when John stated the facts.

"Oh you did huh?" said Marylou. "Well it ain't back there now. What time did you drop it there?"

"Couldn't have been later than 10:30," said John.

Jeff kept on nodding and hoping that N.V. and Marylou would feel even more indebted to them after learning they did the deed they were asked to do in a timely fashion.

"Come on out back boys," ordered Marylou.

The guys quickly followed Marylou and N.V. toward the kitchen.

Marylou, pointing toward the front door, "that way."

The guys did a fast one-eighty and headed toward the front door. Meantime, N.V. and Marylou charged through the kitchen.

Jeff and John ran flat out around the building to the back of the tavern so as not to keep the girls waiting.

"But we dropped it right here!" said John pointing over towards the dumpster.

"Oh you did huh. Well it ain't right here now," said Marylou.

"Well we done what you asked Marylou. You know I am a man of my word," said John resolutely.

"I don't know you hardly at all," replied Marylou.

" I swear to christ, it was there!" John said.

"I'm sorry, but can I say something?" asked Jeff in his low-talker voice.

Nobody gave him permission, but the three of them stopped and stared at him giving him the floor.

"Maybe somebody took it," offered Jeff.

"Now who in the hell would even know about it Einstein?" Marylou shouted.

"Well hell I don't know. I just know Jeff and me put it there just like we said we would," replied John.

Marylou's instinct told her they were telling the truth.

"Well OK. You gotta figure out where it went and I mean now," Marylou ordered like a little Nazi

"We'll help you any way we can, John said sweetly, you know we will."

"I sure hope so boys because you owe us big time," said Marylou.

John and Jeff said their good-byes and walked back to the truck wondering how they got on Marylou's bad side so fast when they did everything they were asked to do.

"Now we gotta find the gang box?" asked Jeff.

With a new level of sadness and frustration, John replied, "If we ever want to get laid we do."

Calvert County was also called "Culvert County" because it was so full of hills and gullies. Drake used a holler behind his house mostly to hunt in, but would drink beer and shoot guns in it during the summer months. Bubba was sailing down the dirt road to Drakes holler. He felt the big rollback truck swaying with every dip and rock in the road, but because he had a cast iron gut the rough road didn't bother him. He made it to the holler and glanced back through the window to make sure he hadn't lost the box along the way. Nope. It was fine. He hopped out of the truck and got the gang box off the Rollback, but didn't know he was being watched by Johnny who was trying to poach a deer twenty yards away and sixteen feet up an oak tree. "What in the hell is in this box?" wondered

Bubba. Just as he was about to open it Johnny's phone started to ring in his dad's ringtone which was "Dueling Banjos."

"OH SHIT!" yelled Bubba. Banjo music I'm out here! Hell No! He jumped back into his truck and took off up the hill trying to shake the creepy feeling.

Johnny answered the phone. "Dad you will not believe what I just found," he said.

"I need your help with the truck boy," said Reeb.

"It's the box Dad! Bubba just dropped it in the holler," said Johnny.

"Hell Yeah! God damn truck is still broke. I'll grab the big wheeled cart and we can tow it back with the car," Reeb said.

The big wheeled cart had eight inch wheels and a steel frame that Reeb made so he could move engines and other heavy things more easily across different surfaces. The gang box weighed almost as much as a car, but he figured it would work. Reeb threw the cart, ropes, and a floor jack into the car and went down the street. Reeb drove down into the holler and Johnny ran up to him.

"What's the plan?" Johnny asked.

"Jack it up, put the cart under it, and tie it to the car. Just hurry up before someone comes," said Reeb.

Johnny got right on it and tied it to the car in no time. His father waited in the car until he was done. Johnny hopped in the car.

"OK let's go," Johnny said. Reeb slowly pushed the gas.

"Come on girl, you can do it," coaxed Reeb.

The car struggled, but made it out of the holler. Paradise Trailer Park had several big hills in it that they had to go up and down. They made it up the second hill fine and got to their first down-hill. Bang! Reeb almost lost control of the car as something hit it.

"What the hell was that!" said Reeb.

"The gang box hit the back of the car," said Johnny.

"How much slack was there?" asked Reeb.

"Maybe ten foot," said Johnny.

"God damnit boy! There should only be a few inches! Go fix it fast," ordered Reeb.

Johnny hopped out, adjusted the ropes, and got back in.

"The back of the car is smashed up a little and has orange paint on it," Johnny said.

"I can't believe you're my son sometimes," scolded Reeb. I hope no one heard that and see's what we are doing."

They got back to the house and drove a bit deeper into the yard.

"Johnny, I want it untied, painted, and hidden as fast as possible," said Reeb.

"Yes sir. You going to work on the truck?" asked Johnny.

"No. I'm going to bed. See you tomorrow," said Reeb.

Bubba got back to the bar to start collecting for the favor.

"Job is done Drake, now let me have a cold one," said Bubba.

"No problem, said Drake with a little chuckle."

"Strangest thing though, Bubba said as he took a swig of beer. I heard banjo music down in that holler."

"You what! That is real bad. Someone might have saw you," said Drake.

"Don't know. It was dark and I just left. I didn't want no deliverance thing happening to me," said Bubba.

"I'll check it out when I get home, replied Drake. Don't worry."

FIVE

OLD BAY

The following day Junior woke up, came outside, and saw Reeb working on his truck. He walked over to say "hi."

"What's happening Junior," said Reeb.

"Still looking for my box. You haven't seen it have you?" asked Junior.

"Nope. Here comes Dwayne. Ask him," replied Reeb.

Dwayne pulled up towing his boat behind his truck.

"What's happening today guys?" said Dwayne.

"Not much. Have you seen my box?" asked Junior.

"Nope, but I caught a bushel of crabs and I'm going to steam them up if y'all want to come over," said Dwayne.

"Oh hell to the yeah! I can't turn down the Chesapeake Bay's finest offering. I'll grab a cooler of beer and we'll be over," replied Reeb.

Eating crabs in Maryland is a social event that brings people together to eat, drink, and bullshit about whatever is on their mind. The guys sat at the picnic table cracking crabs and shooting the shit. Junior didn't know it, but his copper had paid for the whole thing. The gas for the boat, the crab bait, and the beer that Reeb brought.

"Pass the Old Bay Seasoning and a few crabs," said Junior.

"How was the lockjaw appointment Reeb?" asked Dwayne.

"We had to go to Montgomery County. The traffic is so bad up there. We broke down and I'm pretty sure the homeless people don't just take change and bills. I think one of em' had a card swiper. Strange place," said Reeb.

"I ain't never been and ain't going to that county," said Junior

"You never leave this county," said Dwayne.

"Did you see the loader and crane that Beefeater brought home from work?" asked Junior.

"Beef owes me a favor for fixing his wife's car so he is going to take the crane and stack some cars for me," said Reeb.

"That's one way of getting more crap in your yard," said Dwayne.

Beef is a neighbor of their's who works in the demolition business ripping down old buildings so new ones can be built.

"It's summer time and he and his wife are sleeping on the porch because the air conditioner is broke," said Reeb.

"So let me get this straight - they sleep outside and shit in the house?" said Dwayne.

"Ha-ha-ha, God damn that's funny, said Junior, N.V. came over the other day. God damn that girl was looking good."

"What was she wearing?" asked Reeb.

"Shorts and a white tank top," said Junior.

"Oh man," said Dwayne.

"So what happened?" asked Reeb.

"Not much. She was flirting with me, but shot me down."

Junior hocked a luggie and scratched his ass.

"You know she may be a lesbian," said Junior.

"Yeah, that's it," Dwayne said as he shook his head a little.

"Junior, the only time you're ever going to have a smoking hot body is at your cremation," said Reeb.

"What? Look at this tan line," said Junior, as he turned around and pulled his pants down a little.

"Getting your ass half tanned from your ass always showing when you're bent over doesn't count Junior," said Dwayne.

At the entrance to the trailer park was the Posh Salon across the street from Miss Pritchett's, who had the women on high alert watching the neighborhood for the box of copper.

"Junior and Reeb are at Dwayne's eating crabs. All we have to do is distract Mike so we can search Reeb's junk yard. N.V. Go flirt with him while Marylou goes and checks for the box," said Cindy.

"What do I say to him?" asked N.V.

"Well he is gardening. Talk to him about that," said Cindy.

"He knows I don't care about his lawn," said N.V.

"Ask him about the last hockey game he played or tell him you'll wash his riding lawn mower in a bikini for five bucks. Make something up and just do it," said Cindy.

N.V. went over to Mike's and Marylou circled around to approach Reeb's house from behind. She hopped the fence and started looking around the junk piles until she came across the camouflaged painted box. She lifted the lid and saw the copper gleaming in the sun. "Oh, you don't get opportunities like this very often," she thought. She pulled her phone out of her pocket, hopped up on the edge of the gang box, slid down, and laid on the copper wire, fixed her hair, and took a selfie with a big smile on her face. She then took some thinner wire and made a necklace and bracelet and snapped another selfie. "This is fun, she thought. I'm going to cuddle a piece of wire like a baby. This is going to be great. I look pretty good in that first picture. This is going to be my new cover photo on Facebook."

She got out of the box and one by one, she pulled out ten piece's of thick copper wire and shut the box.

"Oh my god this stuff is heavy," she said.

She tried to run out of the yard, but her grip was loosening on the heavy wire, and piece after piece began to fall on the ground. In a panic, she left them there and returned to the Posh Salon.

"I've found it!", Marylou shouted.

"Three pieces is all you found?" asked Cindy.

"No, I dropped some, but I found the box and there's a lot in it," said Marylou, look at the pictures I took.

"Holy shit. It looks beautiful," said Cindy.

"What about me?" asked Marylou.

Yes, the one with the copper jewelry is cute. Wait - you didn't post it on Facebook did you?" asked Cindy.

"I had to," said Marylou.

"Take those down before someone sees them!" ordered Cindy. If you dropped some, Reeb will know someone was there. If it's on Facebook people may start showing up out of nowhere."

N.V. walked into the salon and went into the back room. A minute later she emerged with in her bikini.

"What are you doing?" Cindy asked.

"I'm going to wash Mike's lawn tractor in my bikini for twenty bucks, said N.V., be back soon," as she snapped the waist band then smacked her butt.

"That guy doesn't stand a chance, said Marylou. That ass of hers almost turned me."

"Now take those pictures down," said Cindy.

"Do I have to? I already have twenty likes," said Marylou.

"For now, yes. Until this is over," said Cindy.

Cindy could see Miss Pritchett waving for her from the front porch to come see her.

"I will be back," said Cindy to Marylou.

Cindy walked over and sat on Miss Pritchett's front porch.

"How can I help you Miss Pritchett?" asked Cindy.

"I need bingo money. What is your plan to get that

copper?" asked Miss Pritchett.

"I'm not sure right now," replied Cindy.

"Well think of something fast before Reeb takes the whole box to the scrap yard," said Miss Pritchett. "Oh and by the way, what the hell is N.V. doing?"

"She's washing Mike's tractor for twenty buck," replied Marylou.

Miss Pritchett furrowed her brow and and shook her head disapprovingly.

"I can't just stuff it in my bra. It weighs thousands of pounds," said Cindy.

"You girls will figure it out," said Miss Pritchett.

"Yeah, O.K.," replied Cindy.

Cindy walked back over to the salon.

"What's the plan?" asked Marylou.

"Watch and wait for an opportunity I guess," said Cindy.

N.V. came walking back into Posh.

"That was an easy twenty bucks," said N.V.

"What is he like?" asked Marylou.

"He's a nice guy," replied N.V.

"Did he ask you out?" asked Cindy.

"He stopped just short of that," replied N.V.

"What does he do for a living or where is he from?" asked Cindy.

"I don't know but I'm going to change and go back over there," said N.V.

"What are you going to wear?" asked Marylou.

"My fishing clothes. He's going to be an easy catch," replied N.V. with a little smile.

Junior, Reeb, and Dwayne were finishing up crabs.

"Man, I read in the paper once that some guys would walk into the will-call of the electrical supply house and if no one was there, just grab whatever copper wire was laying around and run out the door," said Dwayne.

"That's bold," said Reeb.

"Holy shit look over there," said Junior.

"Oh hell yes!" said Reeb. N.V. was now in a little dress and stripper shoes.

"I would love to be in Mike's shoes right now," said Dwayne.

"O.K. guys, I have shit to do. I'll see you later," said Reeb.

"Take it easy Reeb," said Junior.

"Do you want to go crabbing Junior?" asked Dwayne.

"No. I have to go deal with that ground hog," said Junior.

"If you finally get him, I'll take it for crab bait," said Dwayne.

"Sure thing. I have a plan today. I'll talk to you later," said Junior.

SIX

BEEFEATER

In a small town, news good and bad, travels fast. The high price of copper can change someone's life, at least for a short while. Beefeater worked in the demolition trade ripping old buildings down. Anything in the building that is worth money is part of the contract. Steel, aluminum, and copper all went to the company. Beefeater wasn't allowed to keep any for himself. He had gotten his name from his backyard wrestling days. Beef, a large, muscular guy, was terrible with money. He lived in a double-wide trailer with his wife Jinx. This affectionate pet name came from their courting days when they would frequently say the same thing at the same time and the first person to say "jinx", owed the other person a Coke. The nickname stuck.

The double-wide had some condition issues. The roof leaked, the air conditioning was broken and Beef didn't care. In the side yard, he had what he called "the guest house." It was a broken down school bus that he ran an electrical service to from the house. It had a partition in the back for sleeping quarters, a small wood stove, a couple window air conditioners that hung off the side, carpeting, a refrigerator, and T.V.'s. He mainly used it when his wife kicked him out of the house and she despised it because it was nicer inside than their actual home. They had an old wooden outhouse in their yard near an old tobacco barn. Beefeater had an old ticker-tape machine next to his chair so he could keep up on current metal prices.

"Beef," Jinx said, "Drake is on the phone."

"OK, thanks," replied Beef.

"Bird, what's going on?" asked Beefeater

"How would you like to help me steal back a box of number 1 copper," asked Drake.

"How much are we talking?" asked Beef.

"A whole gang box full of it. It's a long story, but I think it's at Reeb's from the Facebook picture I just saw," said Drake.

"I have a plan. Get your ass over here," ordered Beefeater.

He ran back to his chair and checked the most current price for copper on the commodities market index. Holy shit, he said to Jinx. "We're talking thousands of dollars. Oh I'm getting a new truck."

"Or you could fix the damn roof so I don't have to watch my shows with a pot on my belly whenever it rains," replied Jinx.

"You would like that wouldn't you? I have to go," Beefeater announced and slammed the door behind him.

"Hey Reeb! You still want me to move some cars around your yard with the crane?" asked Beefeater.

"Yes. I need some room to work around here. Can you take these two and stack them up on a couple of the cars off to the side?" asked Reeb.

Drake came pulling up in his hatch-back beater of a car.

"Hey guys, what's happening?" asked Drake.

"Moving some cars in a few minutes," replied Beefeater. "Want to help?"

"Sure thing," said Drake.

"Get the heavy lifting straps out of the box while I extend the boom. We are picking up the Camry and putting it on the Datsun, and the Taurus is going on top of the K car," instructed Beefeater.

Drake dragged the big straps over to the Camry and started looking around for the gang box. He wrapped one strap around the front end of the car and one around the rear. Beefeater swung the boom over and lowered the cable down. Drake hopped up on the car and attached the straps to the hook and jumped off the car.

"Stand back just in case the car falls," yelled Beefeater.

Drake started looking for the gang box again while Reeb wasn't watching. Meanwhile, Beefeater raised the car up and swung it over. He lowered it a bit too fast and it smashed the Datsun.

"Sorry Reeb! My bad," said Beefeater.

"I don't give a shit," yelled Reeb.

Drake ran over to Beefeater. "I found it!" said Drake.

"Good. Now we just need the right opportunity. Get the straps off that car and get them on the next one. Take this smaller strap with you for the gang box," said Beefeater.

Hey Reeb. Do you have a couple cold ones," asked Beefeater.

"Yeah. I have to drop a deuce first," said Reeb.

"Dropping a couple kids off at the pool huh?" Beefeater shot back.

Reeb walked into the house and Beefeater swung the boom over to the gang box and lowered the cable, while Drake tied the strap around the gang box and attached it to the cable. Beefeater raised it up and started swinging it over to his yard when the strap broke and the gang box fell with a heart-stopping crash on the back of Drake's car.

"God damnit!", yelled Drake.

Drive it home before we get caught," said Beefeater.

"Why did you have me use that piece of shit strap?" yelled Drake.

You have another car. You were the rigger. It was your job to inspect it," said Beefeater.

Drake hopped in the half crushed car. The gang box was sticking out of the rear window. Part of the roof was bent in, but fortunately, not on the driver's side of the car. Drake looked through the cracked windshield and hit the gas.

Beefeater boomed back to the car and lowered the cable. He quickly finished attaching the straps and attached it to the cable. He ran back to the crane, lifted the car, and swung it. He lowered it so fast onto the other car that it smashed the roof and windows out of the K car.

Reeb came walking out of the house and immediately started yelling, "What in the hell is going on out here!"

"Sorry again Reeb," said Beefeater.

"Where is Drake?" asked Reeb.

He got a call from sweetie-pie and had to run home," said Beefeater.

"Here's your beer," said Reeb, annoyed with the typical relationship bullshit.

"Drake wants me to take the loader down to his house and move some shit around, so I can't stay long," said Beefeater.

Just then, Drake came speeding down the road past them.

"Where is he going?" asked Reeb.

"Back to Mira-A-Lago, I think. I have to go get some shit done," said Beefeater.

Miss Pritchett called Cindy. "That gang box is at Drake's house. I saw Beef and Drake take it," she said.

"No shit! I'll get the girls," replied Cindy.

"Do not screw this up this time," scolded Miss Pritchett.

Beefeater climbed up in the loader and drove down to Drake's house. The broken strap was still on the gang box. Beefeater drove up to the car, curled the bucket of the loader forward and tied the strap to the hook on the bucket. He lifted it up and curled the gang box right into the bucket, then headed back to his house. Beefeater drove over to his John boat duck blind in his front yard. Thinking that would conceal the box enough, he dropped the gang box behind the boat, parked the loader, and jumped down. He caught sight of Junior out in his yard with a twenty-two pistol.

"Junior! What are you doing!" yelled Beefeater.

"A ground hog dug his burrow in my favorite dog's grave so I'm going to throw some smoke bombs down his hole, and when he comes up I'm going to blast him," replied Junior.

"Be careful man," said Beefeater.

Junior lit a smoke bomb and tossed it down the hole and stood back. Smoke started billowing out of the hole. The ground hog ran out of the hole right through Junior's legs. It startled him so much he shot and grazed his own leg.

"Oh shit! That hurt!" as he lay there grasping his leg.

Reeb was in his driveway laughing hysterically at the scene.

"Honey, be back in awhile. I got to take Junior to the hospital," said Beefeater to Jinx.

Beefeater walked over to Junior lying on the ground holding his leg.

"That's going to leave a mark Junior," said Beef.

"It's not that bad," said Junior.

"I would pay to see that again," said Beef chuckling.

"That was just a warning shot. That hog won't be back," said Junior.

"Yeah. Right," nodded Beef.

"Come on boy, he said as he picked him up off the ground. Get in the truck," said Beefeater calmly.

"Sorry Beef," said Junior.

SEVEN

IT'S GO TIME

Nothing is more memorable than a first kiss. Mike and N.V. had been eye-balling each other for awhile. Mike was new to the area and quite different than the rest of the residents. It was going to be a hot day and N.V. had on her smallest outfit. She walked over to Mike's trailer while he was watering the grass.

"How are you doing handsome," said N.V.

"Oh my god you look good," replied Mike.

"Thank you. Do you have some sweet tea?" asked N.V.

"Sweet tea for a sweet girl. Sure do. It's in the trailer," Mike replied happily.

The couple walked inside and Mike poured a couple glasses of iced tea and started talking.

"Where are you from?" asked N.V.

"Up north," replied Mike.

"So why did you move to this trailer park?" asked N.V.

"The government made me move here," said Mike.

"You work for the government?" asked N.V.

"Something like that," replied Mike.

"That's mysterious," said N.V.

"When are you going to let me take you to dinner?" asked Mike.

"Whenever you want," said N.V.

She took a piece of ice out of her glass and started slowly rubbing it on her upper chest to cool off. Mike couldn't take it anymore and reached out and put his hands around her waist, pulling her to him. Their lips met and their hands and arms wrapped around each other. Mike began kissing her neck.

"Oh god," moaned N.V.

Mike felt a little bump on her neck and pulled back.

"What's the matter?" asked N.V.

"There is something on you neck," said Mike.

N.V. felt the bump and quickly pulled it off.

"Just a tick," she said.

"Are you going to be OK?" asked Mike in a concerned manner.

"I will when you start kissing me again," N.V. replied.

Mike didn't think twice and immediately started kissing her again.

N.V.'s phone started ringing and she pulled it out of her pocket.

"It's Cindy. I have to take this," said N.V.

Mike sighed.

"What do you want? I'm busy!" said N.V.

"We have work to do I need you to come to the salon," replied Cindy.

"OK. I'll be there in a minute," replied N.V.

"I have to go handsome, but I will see you again soon and we'll get that dinner," said N.V. sweetly leading him on.

"I can't wait!" said Mike.

N.V. gave him a little kiss goodbye and headed out the door. She walked into the salon and saw Cindy at the window peering through her binoculars.

"What's going on Cindy?" asked N.V.

"Long story short, Beef and Drake just stole the box from Reeb. Beef then went and stole it from Drake and Reeb has no idea from the looks of it," explained Cindy.

Marylou ran into the salon, over-heated from the short jog because it was so muggy you could see the haze in the air.

"Drake has the box, I think," Marylou informed.

"Not anymore he doesn't, said Cindy, Beef and Junior left together, Dwayne is crabbing, I think, so all we have to do is distract Reeb."

"Where is Beefeater's wife?" asked N.V.

"I saw her leave too but I'm not sure to where or when she's coming back," said Cindy.

"What is our plan?" asked Marylou.

"N.V. - we need Reeb to go to the far side of his property so he isn't near the box. N.V., take your car over to the next street and fake a breakdown. Ask him to take a look at it so we have a little time," Cindy explained clearly.

"Got it!" said N.V.

She hopped in her car and drove to the next street, pulled over, popped the hood, and pulled a wire off a spark plug. Cindy watching the whole time. N.V. started to call Reeb and Cindy could see him walking around to go help her.

"The plan's working," Cindy informed Marylou.

"Marylou, I want you to take that fifty gallon blue barrel that is strapped to the hand truck and take it up there and fill it up," said Cindy.

"Roger that," replied Marylou.

Marylou went down the street and quickly hid behind the boat. She opened the gang box and started filling the barrel with copper. Cindy watched her fill it, close the gang box lid and try to move the barrel. She was struggling with the weight and couldn't get it to budge.

"God damn it. There is always a problem," yelled Cindy.

She grabbed her keys and ran out to her minivan. She sped over to Marylou, jumped out, and opened the rear door.

"Together. One, two, three. Holy crap this is heavy," said Cindy.

They managed to tilt it back, get it on two wheels and over to the car.

"Put the handles on the back of the car and hop in. We'll tow it back," said Cindy.

Marylou sat in the back of the car trying to hold onto the hand truck as best she could as Cindy drove them up the hill and back to the salon.

A hundred yards away, N.V. could see them pull up at the salon. Reeb popped the plug wire back on and shut the hood.

"Thank you so much," said N.V. as she hopped into the car and fired it up.

"Yeah, no problem," said Reeb as he watched her drive away.

The girls had forgotten about one person - Johnny, who was watching them and saw their whole operation. He really wanted a piece of the copper money all to himself.

Reeb walked back through his yard and saw a piece of copper wire laying in the wasteland. He walked over and picked it up. There were smaller foot prints that could only be from a woman's shoe. heading in the direction of the salon. He could see the girls unloading the contents of a blue barrel into Cindy's minivan.

"What the hell is going on around here," said Reeb thinking out loud.

He walked over to where he hid the gang box only to find it missing. He started to turn red with anger and quickly walked back to the house.

"Johnny! Get out here!" he hollered.

"Yeah Dad," said Johnny.

"The damn gang box is gone. There were girl's footprints, but they couldn't have taken the whole god damned box. It was too heavy. Beef could have, but I had my eyes on him almost the whole time. I want you to get that whole bag of Roman Candles and put them all over the yard. Wire them up to three separate electronic igniters," ordered Reeb.

"What is the switch?" asked Johnny.

"We'll use motion sensors," said Reeb.

"I have to go to the hardware store and pick one more up," said Johnny, trying to be helpful to his father.

"Whatever!" I am sick of these thieves," said Reeb.

"We did steal it first," reminded Johnny.

"Whatever! Just hurry up!" said Reeb as he walked into the house hot and disgusted.

Seeing his opportunity, Johnny grabbed an old rickety wheel barrow and ran across the street to Beefeater's yard. He located the gang box and started chucking copper into the wheel barrow. He closed the box and started to make his way back. Driving up the road, was Dwayne pulling his boat. Johnny started running as fast as he could toward his yard. Dwayne could see who it was as he was driving past.

The front wheel on the wheel barrow suddenly broke off and the front snow-plowed into the dirt sending Johnny flipping over it and landing on his back with the wheel barrow on top of him. All Dwayne could see was his feet flying up in the air like a cartoon.

"Oh man, that must have hurt, said Dwayne to himself, I wonder what he was doing."

Johnny lay on the ground in pain, but quickly picked himself up and loaded the copper into his car and took off for the scrap yard.

Dwayne parked his boat and put his crabs in a cooler. He hopped on his old four wheeler and went to find out what that kid was doing. He got close to the boat and hit the gas a little more and the throttle stuck. Dwayne went flying by the boat barely catching a glimpse of the gang box, ran right through Beefeater's old wooden outhouse knocking him off and the four wheeler crashed into the bushes. A vine wrapped around the axle and sucked it up a tree before the vine broke. The four wheeler fell to the ground and flipped down the hill.

"Oh god. That hurt bad. That's going to leave a couple marks, he said as he felt some blood dripping down his face. He picked himself up off the ground and started limping home.

"Someone painted the box, he thought. How did it get where its at?"

It didn't matter. It's there now. Only the copper mattered.

Cindy and the girls pulled into he scrap yard.

"How are you ladies?" asked Mags.

"Oh we are doing just fine," Cindy said as she opened the back of the minivan.

"Now where did you ladies manage to find all this copper?" asked Mags.

"I'm dating an electrician," said Marylou.

"As if it's any of your business," said Cindy.

"Calm down," said Mags.

He unloaded the wire on the scale as they waited. Four hundred, fifty pounds.

"Here is your ticket," said Mags.

"Thank you scrap man. Come on girls let's get our cash," said Cindy.

Johnny pulled into the scrap yard as the girls were leaving.

"Shit! They aren't done yet," he said Johnny not wanting to be seen.

"Another Paradise Trailer Park person," said Mags.

"Hey, what's up?" asked Johnny.

"All that copper coming out of there like you're mining it. Maybe I should move there too," said Mags.

"Some days you just get lucky, said Johnny.

"I haven't got lucky in six months," said Mags as he handed Johnny his ticket.

"Thanks a lot man," said Johnny as he quickly moved along not wanting any chit-chat.

Something is up, thought Mags. It was quitting time so he punched the clock. "I'm going to see Junior."

Johnny returned from the scrap yard and found his dad

running wire all over the yard.

"This is going be awesome. I have all the Roman candles pointed at chest height," said Reeb.

"What do you want me to do?" asked Johnny.

"Finish wiring the motion sensors," replied Reeb.

"This will be a big waste of time if a wild animal sets them off," said Johnny.

"We will burn that bridge when we get there," replied Reeb.

Reeb's gold fever grew by the minute.

EIGHT

THE HIGH WATER MARK

As the day turned into night, the trailer park began to look through blood stained eyes. Copper money got the liquor flowing. Cindy and Marylou were four shots deep at the salon and having a reflective moment.

"Every time we have to split our take four ways with that old woman it is bad for business," said Cindy.

"Uh-huh. Well if you want to make another run at the copper, we had better keep an eye out," replied Marylou.

Beefeater brought Junior back from the hospital.

"Thanks a lot man," said Junior appreciatively.

"Seeing you do it was worth the time I spent waiting in the Emergency Room," replied Beef with a big fat grin.

Junior slid out of the truck and began slowly limping towards his house when Chrome Mags pulled up and hopped out of his car.

"Hey Cousin. What happened to you?" asked Mags.

"I accidentally shot myself trying to kill a ground hog," said Junior.

"Ha-Ha-Ha-Ha, god damn that's funny," hollered Mags.

"I'll get that damn hog," said Junior.

"Got any whiskey?" asked Mags.

"Hell yeah."

Junior grabbed a bottle and poured a couple shots. The two slammed them back and poured another.

"Is their gold in these hills?" asked Mags.

"What are you talking about?" replied Junior.

"You, Johnny, and them girls have all brought copper in lately," informed Mags.

"Lock Jaw Johnny? Those bitches? God damn it!" yelled Junior.

"What?" said Mags

"I had a big ass gang box full of copper but someone stole it. I need your help to get it back," said Junior.

"You are talking big money. Oh I'm in," replied Mags.

"It has to be close," said Junior.

Mags and Junior threw back another shot of whiskey and went over a plan.

"Do you have another gang box?" asked Mags.

"Yes, but why?" asked Junior.

"I will create a diversion. You start pushing that box down the road and maybe whoever has it will think you're taking it from them," said Mags.

"That's not a bad idea," said Junior.

"Give me twenty of them smoke bombs," said Mags.

"Why?" asked Junior.

"Give me two minutes. I will head up wind, walk down the street dropping them in a line over on the next street. The smoke will blow right over to you," said Mags.

"Won't they look at you?" asked Junior.

"Maybe. That gang box should make plenty of noise so they will see you," said Mags.

"O.K. Cool," said Junior.

Mags grabbed twenty smoke bombs and headed upwind of Junior. Meanwhile, Junior rolled the gang box out of the shed and out to the road.

"Cindy, something is going on out here. Junior has a gang box out by the road," said Marylou.

"Did he get it from beef?" asked Cindy.

"No," replied Marylou.

"Keep an eye on him," said Cindy.

On the next street, Mags started lighting smoke bombs and dropping them as he walked and Junior started pushing the gang box down the street. Smoke started covering the neighborhood.

"Is there a fire?" yelled Reeb as he leaped up from out of his chair. Johnny, I think there is a fire," Reeb said as he ran outside.

Beefeater saw the smoke and quickly ran out into his yard.

Reeb saw Junior pushing the box down the smokey street and ran down to the end of his driveway. Junior started running and got to the top of the big hill in the neighborhood, hopped on top and started riding it down the hill.

"Oh shit!" yelled Junior, "this was really stupid."

The box picked up speed as it careened down the hill. Two of the pivot wheels spun the box around so Junior was now heading feet first. The gang box hit a pot hole and threw Junior to the side skidding across the pavement. The box flipped end over end and came to a rest. Reeb ran down the hill until he got to Junior. He looked at the broken box and saw it did not have any copper in it.

"Junior! What the hell are you doing?"Are you trying to kill yourself?" exclaimed Reeb.

"Oh my god that hurt," said Junior.

"I bet it did. What were you doing?" asked Reeb.

"Started drinking whiskey and the idea of riding down the hill sounded fun," said Junior as he picked himself up off the asphalt.

Beefeater, thinking something was up, hid in the yard. Smoke still filled the air as Cindy and Marylou came out of the salon, grabbed an old shopping cart that was close by, and started heading towards Beefeater's. Mags was creeping around, looking in yards and heard the shopping cart the girls were pushing, so he took cover. In the darkness, he scanned the area and then started running through the smoke into Beefeater's yard. Beefeater stepped out and clothes-lined Mags. Mags hit the ground with a thud. Then Beefeater dropped an elbow on Mag's chest that The Rock would have been proud of. Beef quickly got back to his feet. Mags was gasping for air when Beefeater grabbed him by his shirt and the back of his pants, picked him up and threw him out into the street. The girls saw the fight going on and ran to take cover in Reeb's yard. As they ran into Reeb's yard, they tripped one of the motion sensors, lighting some of the roman candles. Rockets flew through the air in rapid succession with plumes of smoke and loud booms.

"What the hell is going on?" screamed Marylou.

"We gotta get out of here!" yelled Cindy.

Reeb heard the fireworks and started running back up the hill towards home. Cindy and Marylou hauled ass back to the salon.

Reeb's yard look like a scene from "Platoon." Just then, Johnny ran out of the house and met his dad.

"Who is in the yard?" yelled Reeb.

"I don't know," replied Johnny.

"Well let's fan out and find him," ordered Reeb.

The two started looking around the old cars and metal, but almost immediately set off another two sensors lighting the other roman candles. Explosions started happening all around them, so Reeb hit the dirt and began belly crawling. A startled raccoon jumped out of an old trash can and landed right on Reeb's face.

"Aahhh shit! Johnny, help me!" hollered Reeb.

Johnny ran over to his dad.

"Holy shit," said Johnny.

"Get this thing off of me!" yelled Reeb as he wrestled with the raccoon.

Johnny grabbed a two by four, cocked back ready to swing, but was hit in the chest by one of the roman candles and the explosion knocked him to the ground. Reeb smashed his head and the raccoon into a car hood and it finally let go. Reeb fell back onto the ground holding his face.

"Oh god," said Reeb.

Johnny picked himself up off the ground, looked at his father, and exclaimed "that thing scratched your face all up."

"It hurts," cried Reeb.

"Oh shit dad. One of the roman candles lit a car on fire," informed Johnny.

"God damnit!" yelled Reeb. "Let's get the fire extinguishers."

Junior limped back up the hill and saw Mags holding his chest.

"What happened to you?" asked Junior.

"I'm really not sure. I was running then something laid me out," said Mags.

"There is a fire at Reeb's," said Mags.

"Let's go check it out," said Junior.

Junior and Mags staggered over to Reeb's where they were quickly joined by Beefeater.

"Just let it burn," said Junior.

"What happened to you?" asked Mags.

"A raccoon attacked me," said Reeb.

"No means no," said Beef.

"What happened to me? Look at Junior! He looks like shit. Gun shot wound. Road rash. I think you have a piece of gravel stuck in your forehead," said Reeb.

"What was all the explosions?" asked Beef.

"Just me and Johnny having fun is all," said Reeb.

Seeing everyone distracted, the girls seized the moment and grabbed the grocery cart again and headed back to get some copper. They crept into Beefeater's yard, opened the box and began to fill their cart.

"Did you hear something?" Cindy asked Marylou.

Cindy turned around and Dwayne was standing there with a toboggan.

"Well this is awkward ladies," said Dwayne.

"What are you doing here?" asked Cindy.

"Maybe I should ask you the same thing," replied Dwayne.

Dwayne reached into the box and started grabbing wire. The girls finished filling their shopping cart.

"Agree that we didn't see each other," said Cindy.

"Ageed," replied Dwayne quickly.

Cindy and Marylou ran back to the salon both pushing the shopping cart like a couple little girls. Miss Pritchett, who had been wakened by the fireworks, caught sight of them running with the squeaky cart.

The sheriff pulled into the trailer park, pulled up close to the devastation, and confronted Beefeater, Mags, Junior, Reeb, and Johnny.

"OK you guys. What the hell are you doing now?" yelled Sheriff Moran.

Reeb and Johnny sprayed the fire with the extinguishers just to look like responsible citizens in front of the sheriff.

"Move along. Nothing to see here," said Beefeater.

"I can't keep coming down here once a week because you people are doing something else crazy," said Sheriff Moran.

"I don't know what you're talking about," said Junior.

"What happened to you Junior?" asked the sheriff, "You're bleeding."

"Allegedly," said Junior.

"No! That's a fact," said the sheriff.

"I get that word mixed-up too," said Mags.

"O.K., it's getting late and I would like it if you would all go home and let the county get some sleep," said Sheriff Moran.

"Allegedly, I may have rabies," said Reeb.

"I could believe that," said the sheriff.

"Why are you always hassling us?" asked Junior.

"Because out of the whole county, I get the most complaints about this one little area," replied Sheriff Moran.

"We didn't do nothing," said Reeb.

"Let's say I believe that. Can you all keep it down for the rest of the night?" asked Sheriff Moran.

"You are asking a lot," said Beef.

"Just keep it down," replied the Sheriff as he got in his car and drove away.

"Guys, I have to nurse some injuries. I'm going home," said Junior.

"See you guys later," said Beefeater, " I think everybody's had enough for one night."

NINE

RED IN THE MORNING

N.V. and Mike were having drinks at Mar-A-Lago Tavern. Drake had a little problem of drinking with the customers. It was getting close to closing time. N.V. and Mike stood at the bar feeling quite good with his arm around her waist, whispering sweet somethings into her ear.

"Have one more shot of Jameson with me," said Drake.

"Line em' up," said N.V.

"Close out our tab too," said Mike.

"Don't worry about that. I'll get the check," N.V. said sweetly, " I got some copper money today."

"Wait. What?" said Drake as he drank his shot of whiskey.

"What is copper money?" asked Mike.

"We sold some copper at the scrap yard," said N.V.

"Did you get that from Reeb?" asked Drake.

"Nope," giggled N.V.

"You make a living in the strangest ways," said Mike.

Drake began to stew.

"Did you get it from Beef?" asked Drake.

"Maybe we did," giggled N.V.

"O.K. That was last call and we are closing," said Drake abruptly as he turned on all the lights.

"Oh alright," said N.V., I want to get this man home."

"Yeah, I bet you do," muttered Drake under his breath.

Mike smiled real big and patted her butt as they went towards the door. Drake threw back another shot and sloppily wiped down the bar.

Reeb was still up drinking and talking with Johnny, getting angrier and angrier.

"Johnny, I swear I'm going to start water boarding people until I get some answers. We need that copper!" hollered Reeb.

"It's three in the morning Dad. I gotta go to bed," replied Johnny, who was getting weary of his father's drunken rant.

"Our financial future is in jeopardy and you want to sleep," Reeb exclaimed.

"A few thousand dollars is not our future and that box isn't going to magically appear," replied Johnny in a matter of fact tone of voice.

"There is that," conceded Reeb.

"Johnny, you're coming with me. We are going on a stake-out," said Reeb.

"Shit," Johnny thought to himself, "I was inches from a clean get-away."

"What the hell are you talking about?" stated Johnny.

"We are going to sit up in one of those cars that Beef stacked-up and wait till we see the box," said Reeb.

"God damnit!" replied Johnny.

Johnny knew where the box was, but was afraid that his dad would confiscate the money he got earlier that day, so he went along with it once again.

Reeb grabbed a cooler and loaded it up with beer saying, "This is probably an eight beer job." He judged the length of something he was doing by how many beers he would drink doing it and not run out. Reeb and Johnny walked out into the yard and climbed up into the car Beef stacked for him. Drake pulled into the trailer park and when he got near Beefeater's house, he drove past real slow.

"That's Drake!" said Reeb.

"He's driving slower than normal alright," observed Johnny.

"What time is it now?" asked Reeb in a slurred voice.

"Just after four. What the hell is that smell?" asked Johnny.

"Sorry boy, I farted," said Reeb.

Johnny quickly rolled down the window and gasped for air.

After a couple hours of waiting, Beefeater's light came on.

"Suspect number two," said Reeb.

"You suspect everyone," replied Johnny.

"And for good reason," replied Reeb.

Beefeater came out of his house and started the crane. Then he did his pre-trip inspection then went to check on the gang box. As he got closer, he could see that lid of the gang box was not shut all the way and he ran over to it.

"Shit! I have to hide it better." He gritted his teeth and pushed it over and into the tobacco barn, shut the door, hopped into the crane, and went to work. A red sky started lighting up the neighborhood.

"I knew Beef stole it," said Reeb as he climbed down from the car.

Johnny hopped out of the passenger side.

"Whatever you're thinking, it's a bad idea," said Johnny.

"And why is that?" asked Reeb.

"Red sky at night, sailor's delight. Red in the morning…," Johnny recited.

Reeb cut Johnny off, "Fuck that warning," he replied.

"Get the cable off the jack car just like before. When you're ready just give the cable a tug," ordered Reeb.

"Yeah. Sure," replied Johnny.

Johnny grabbed the cable and ran across the street, but he heard something moving at the back of the barn, so he crouched down next to a set of farm discs. Drake came sneaking in the back of the barn, saw the gang box, and ran to it.

"Oh Baby, I found you again! I'll go get the car," said Drake out loud as he spoke to the gang box as it was a real life person.

He closed the box and went back out of the barn. Johnny stood back up and pulled the cable to get more slack. Reeb saw the cable get pulled and hit the gas. The cable pulled out of Johnny's hands, caught on the discs and it rolled smoothly out of the barn.

"Oh shit," Johnny thought. He watched as the discs picked up speed going across the street. The discs hit a bump and the cable came off, but it was moving so fast it smashed into the back of the jack car knocking it off it's blocks, Reeb was still on the gas as the wheels hit the ground sending Reeb driving through the yard, smashing into another car and driving onto its hood. Reeb's chest hit the steering wheel. Johnny ran across the street to help his dad. Reeb opened the door and fell out of the car.

"Oh god. That hurt," said Reeb.

"Are you O.K.?" asked Johnny.

"Hell no, I'm not O.K.! What the hell just happened?" asked Reeb

"More than one accident at a time. Drinking and driving isn't a good idea even if it's in your own yard," said Johnny.

"Get away from me," said Reeb still lying in the dirt.

Johnny walked into the house and shut the door. Just then Drake pulled up and backed into the barn. Reeb struggled to get back to his feet. Still drunk and awake for twenty nine hours straight, he stared at the discs.

"That stupid kid. Now if we had a tractor we could make a garden," Reeb said disgusted.

Reeb heard an engine fire up and saw Drake's car come out of the barn and drive past him. He started running across his yard dodging debris and yelling at Drake.

"Get back here you son of a bitch!" Reeb shouted.

Reeb ran around a car at the edge of his property next to the street and hit his head on a pipe that was sticking out of the passenger side window, knocking him unconscious.

"Ha-Ha-Ha-Ha," laughed Mike who was watching out his window.

"What is it?" asked N.V.

"That idiot Reeb just knocked himself out in his own yard. Look you can see his feet sticking out from his yard next to that old wrecked car," laughed Mike.

"He is pretty wild," said N.V.

"You look really cute in my shirt. Do you want breakfast?" asked Mike.

N.V. pulled the shirt up showing nothing but her bare ass.

"Maybe you want to go back to bed," said N.V.

"Let's go woman," said Mike.

"Wait. Cindy is calling," said N.V."

"Don't answer it," Mike said as he pulled her towards the bedroom.

"She's not answering," said Cindy.

"She's in love," said Marylou.

"Shit. Miss Pritchett is calling," said Marylou.

"Hello Miss Pritchett," said Cindy cheerfully.

"Did you cash that cart full of copper in yet?" asked Miss Pritchett.

"What cart full of copper?" replied Cindy.

"Don't play dumb with me. I saw you and Marylou running back to the salon during all that commotion over at Reeb's house last night," said Miss Pritchett angrily.

"Oh yes. We were just about to," said Cindy.

"Unless you want your rent to go up on the salon, I expect my cut. I still own that building," said Miss Pritchett as she hung up the phone.

"Let's go to the scrap yard Marylou."

TEN

HOT & STICKY

The humidity of a Maryland summer can make it feel like your breath is being taken away. Today was one of those days. Hot, muggy, hazy, and miserable. Severe storms are predicted daily and are normally fast moving. Dwayne and Junior had just come back from crabbing, as evil looking dark cloud were forming in the western sky. They were hot and thirsty as well as reeking of sweat and crab bait.

"Let's get the crabs in the cooler till the storm blows by," said Dwayne.

"Alright. We need to get some beer iced down," said Junior.

"Way ahead of you Junior," Let's watch the storm in the shed," replied Dwayne.

Dwayne and Junior walked into the shed and Dwayne opened-up a small refrigerator and tossed Junior a beer. Junior grabbed the beer out of the air and grabbed a couple pop-up chairs. The thunder and lighting was filling the sky. Rain started coming down hard.

"I hope we get to see something get hit by lightening," said Junior as he settled down to watch the storm.

"I'm glad we knocked-off crabbing when we did," said Dwayne, "I hate getting stuck on the water during an electrical storm."

Beefeater pulled up in front of his house in the crane and ran inside and got his wife.

"Honey, come with me," said Beef.

"What's wrong?" she asked.

"There might be a tornado. Let's get in the crane," said Beef.

She grabbed her coat and purse, and ran out to the crane.

"What are they doing?" asked Dwayne.

"Maybe they are going to have sex in the crane," said Junior.

"Romantic devil," said Dwayne.

"Are you seeing what I'm seeing?" asked Junior.

"I can't see in their windows. They're too far away," said Dwayne.

"I think that's a funnel cloud! Oh shit! What do we do?" yelled Junior.

"Hide under the car," shouted Dwayne.

The tornado touched-down briefly in Juniors yard causing part of his trailer to collapse. It quickly spun back up in the sky and then came back down completely destroying Beefeater's old barn, and then touched-down into the woods dropping trees. After a few minutes, the rain and the wind began to settle down. Beefeater jumped out of the crane and ran to what was left of his barn.

"Oh no!" The storm took the box," cried Beef.

His wife walked back to the house feeling a little dizzy and confused.

"I wish it would have taken that bus," she yelled.

A storm team helicopter from a local Washington, D.C. television network that was following the storm now hovered overhead.

"Can you see these camera shots? The path of destruction is horrible. Debris is everywhere," said the cameraman in the chopper.

"Does it look like everyone is O.K.," asked the reporter.

"It's hard to say. Our news truck is pulling in now," said the cameraman.

The T.V. crew jumped out of the van, grabbed the camera and started recording.

"We are on the scene live to witness this horrible tragedy. A tornado touched down in Calvert County and wait! I think I see a body sticking out of the debris. Do you think that guy is alive?" asked the reporter.

"I don't know. Poke at him with a stick," said the cameraman.

He picked up a stick and poked Reeb in the gut. Reeb popped-up with a gasp of air.

"What the hell happened!" asked Reeb.

"We have a survivor," yelled the reporter.

"Who the hell are you? How did I get all wet?"

asked Reeb.

"Sir, you were in a tornado. It looks like it did terrible damage to your property. It must have touched down and travelled all over your property, picked you up and threw you over here," said the concerned reporter.

"What the hell are you talking about? My yard always looks like this, Wait. What? A tornado?" asked Reeb.

"Sir, you've had a terrible shock. It also hit the neighbor's trailer and the barn," said the reporter.

"The barn! The box! God Damn It! The tragedy we have suffered!" cried Reeb.

"Sir do you want a paramedic?" asked the reporter.

"No I don't. I want a beer," replied Reeb.

Dwayne and Junior walked over to see the reporter.

"I have some more survivors. Sir, you look like you have been through a lot," the reporter said.

"My house is wrecked. The sound of the wind was terrible. Sounded like a freight train," said Junior, as he cracked open another beer.

"Don't worry Junior. I'm calling the insurance company. That tornado picked up my four wheeler and tossed it in the woods," said Dwayne.

"What?" asked Junior.

"Are you serious? We had a tornado. I mean I have damage. I need to make a claim with the insurance company too," said Reeb.

"We'll have your trailer as good as new soon. Anything you need, we will help," said Dwayne.

"When you get that insurance guy on the phone, tell him it happened again," said Junior.

"I got him on the phone. Hey we had another tornado. We need you to come down here and do an assessment," said Dwayne.

"Sir, I keep telling you that your policies don't cover acts of nature," replied the agent.

"Are you saying we can't make a claim?" asked Dwayne.

Junior grabbed the phone out of Dwayne's hands.

"What's this bullshit?" asked Junior.

"You can't make a claim on acts of nature," said the agent.

"What nature. We had a tornado," said Junior.

"You keep calling me with wild stories or accidentally lighting your own property on fire. I realize you can clean lots of the things with gasoline, but you have to stay away from sparks and flame," said the agent.

"You are never there when I need you," said Junior.

"You can't throw an old crapper tank at your car and claim it's space junk," replied the agent.

"Well what about that life insurance policy I was asking about?" asked Junior.

"There is no way I could ever cover you on a life insurance policy. I know you too well, replied the agent. Goodbye!"

"Hello, hello. The fucker hung up on me," exclaimed Junior.

"A community pulling together as one. Let's go talk with this gentleman and his wife. Sir, did you see the tornado?" asked the reporter.

"It was horrible! We hid in the crane for protection and watched it take thousands of dollars from us. Broke our barn and outhouse," said Beef.

"We will definitely be calling the insurance company about the damage to our roof," said Beef's wife as she leaned-in to make sure she got on T.V.

Sheriff Moran pulled into the trailer park and hopped out of the car. "Is everybody O.K.?" asked the Sheriff.

"Don't we look O.K.?" asked Junior.

"Actually no. No you don't, said Sheriff Moran. You look like you have been in a war."

"Sheriff, would you like to make a statement?" asked the reporter.

"Yes. We have some of the most resilient residents here in Calvert County. They will have it rebuilt in no time," said Sheriff Moran.

"Because I'm not going to get a permit," said Junior quietly.

The Sheriff continued, "And if I am elected again this fall,

I will still be serving this great county."

"We have a tornado and he makes time to be a politician," said Reeb.

"That's the latest update from The Storm Team reporting to you live from southern Maryland," said the reporter.

"Thanks a lot everyone for the interviews," said the reporter.

"Hey, me and Junior caught a bushel of crabs. Let's get them steamed-up and on the picnic tables," said Dwayne.

"Now you're talking," said Reeb.

Johnny came outside and joined the gang.

"Look a rainbow," said Johnny.

"That's where my pot of gold is now," said Reeb wistfully.

"Johnny, go get Cindy, Marylou, N.V. and Mike so they can have some crabs," said Reeb.

Junior grabbed a beer and sat down at the picnic table, pulled a scratch off ticket out of his pocket, and started scraping at it with a beer tab. He looked at it twice and then a third time. It was a fifty thousand dollar winner. He put it back in his pocket.

"Did you win Junior?" asked Dwayne.

"Nope. Scratched a whole roll of them and nothing," said Junior.

Junior had learned his lesson on talking trash about his good fortune.